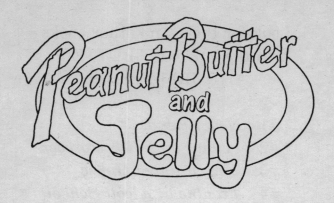

ALCOTT LIBRARY IS
FALLING DOWN

Look for these and other books
in the PEANUT BUTTER
AND JELLY series:

Peanut Butter and Jelly

#9

ALCOTT LIBRARY IS FALLING DOWN

Dorothy Haas

Illustrated by Paul Casale

A
LITTLE APPLE
PAPERBACK

SCHOLASTIC INC.
New York Toronto London Auckland Sydney

ISBN 0-590-43558-2

Copyright © 1991 by Dorothy F. Haas.
All rights reserved. Published by Scholastic Inc.
PEANUT BUTTER AND JELLY is a trademark of Scholastic Inc.
APPLE PAPERBACKS is a registered trademark of Scholastic Inc.

12 11 10 9 8 7 6 5 4 3 2 1   1 2 3 4 5 6/9

Printed in the U.S.A.   40

First Scholastic printing, January 1991

CHAPTER
1

■▬■▬■▬■▬■▬■▬■▬■▬■▬■

Tik. Tik. Tik. Tik. Tik.

Peanut and Jilly were in the Learning Center at Louisa May Alcott School. Mrs. Harris, the librarian, had just finished telling their class about library skills. The Learning Center was bright and cozy. Outdoors, the day was gray. Sheets of rain beat against the windows.

Tik. Tik.

Jilly looked around. What was that noise? It sounded like the ticking of a grandfather clock.

Peanut — properly named Polly Butterman,

but called Peanut by almost everybody — heard the noise, too. She swung around, looking. It sounded like her sister Ceci pecking away on her computer. Only there was no computer here in the Learning Center.

Tik. Tik. Tik. Tik.

Voices rose as everybody started talking about favorite books.

"I like comic books," said Elvis. "Hey — did any of you guys ever wonder what kind of comic books Donald Duck or Woody Woodpecker have? I mean, maybe their comic books have *people* running around doing wild stuff." He doubled over, laughing.

"I've got the first book I ever had," said Carrie. "It's about a little cat. I don't read it anymore, but I like having it."

"I like books about *real* stuff," said David. "Volcanoes and cars and dinosaurs."

Tik.

"Stories are real," said Courtney. "I mean, somebody made one up and there's a book. And you can't forget about the story once you read it. So, stories are real."

Tik. Tik.

2

Where *was* that strange ticking noise coming from!

Jilly looked around the room, frowning. *Tik. Tik.* The noise was the kind that made you pay attention to it.

Peanut was looking, too. Something about the noise said that it did not belong here in the LC.

Jilly spotted a shiny place on the floor that caught the light from overhead. *Tik.* A drop of water splashed onto the wet spot. *Tik. Tik.* She leaped to her feet. "Mrs. Harris! Mrs. Harris! There's — "

Everybody was talking. Mrs. Harris clapped her hands to stop the din. "All right, people. One person at a time. Raise your hands."

"But, Mrs. Harris," gasped Jilly.

"I believe Courtney had her hand up first, Jillian," said Mrs. Harris. Jillian was Jilly's real name, and teachers often called her that. "I will call on you next."

Jilly couldn't wait for her turn. This was an emergency. "Water's coming in," she yelled. "Look! Over there!" She pointed at the puddle.

"Oh, mercy!" gasped Mrs. Harris. She looked around desperately, grabbed a wastebasket, and ran to the puddle. She put the wastebasket in place, looking up at the ceiling. Drops of water hung there about to fall.

The *tik* sound turned into a *ping* . . . *ping* . . . *ping* as water fell into the metal wastebasket.

Talk about favorite books had stopped. The kids were all watching, their eyes round. Suddenly the drops turned into a rush of water. It sounded as though somebody had turned on a faucet.

Mrs. Harris hurried back to her desk. She made shooing motions with her hands. "Off with you all," she said. "Back to your classroom." She picked up the telephone and dialed a number. "Don't run in the hall," she called as everyone rushed toward the door.

But they did run, stomping down the stairs. Something different was happening. Something exciting.

"Maybe there's a leak in the ceiling of our room," said Erin.

"There's going to be a deluge," said David,

who always used big words. He looked like he hoped there *would* be a flood.

"So let's go build a boat," said Peanut, laughing.

"Me first to row," said Jilly, grinning. "I know how to row."

"If we're going to build a boat," said Ollie as they turned the corner on the landing, "let's build — "

He stopped dead in his tracks. So did everybody else. Kids bumped into kids. Mr. Granger was standing in the lower hall, looking up at them. Mr. Granger was the principal of Louisa May Alcott School.

"I think I heard somewhere that running is not allowed in the halls," he boomed. Mr. Granger didn't talk the way other people do — his voice always bounced off the walls. "Have any of you heard that?"

"Yes, Mr. Granger," they all whispered, looking down at their shoes.

"So, okay, walk the rest of the way to your classroom," said Mr. Granger.

He waited, watching them, as they filed past.

Everybody walked. Nobody talked. Nobody said a word until they got into their room and closed the door. Then Ollie finished what he had started to say. " — a submarine. If we're gonna build a boat, let's build a submarine."

Miss Kraft was sitting at her desk, writing. When they poured into the room she lowered her head onto her arms for a moment. "Your library skills class can't be over already," she said, coming up for air. "I thought I was going to get some record-keeping done. Why are you back here so soon?"

They crowded around her desk and told her about the big leak in the Learning Center's ceiling.

"At first it was just a drip."

"But then it came pouring down."

"Mrs. Harris called somebody."

"She told us to go back to our room."

"Jilly's the first one who saw it."

David had been walking around the room, looking up at the ceiling. "No drips here," he said, coming to join the others.

"What will happen to the books in the LC if they get all wet?"

7

"Calm down, everybody," said Miss Kraft. "I'm sure we aren't on the edge of disaster. It's probably just something that's part of the work the roofers have been doing this past week. You can be sure Mr. Larson and the workers will take care of everything."

Mr. Larson was Louisa May Alcott's custodian. He made things run smoothly in and around the building.

"All right, now," said Miss Kraft. "Back to your desks. There's still time to do a little work on your math."

Things quieted down, and they tended to their math. But math problems were a dull way to spend the rest of the afternoon after all the excitement in the Learning Center.

At last the final bell rang, jangling for the longest time. Peanut and Jilly put things in their desks, stuffed their homework into their backpacks, and hurried out into the hall. They sat on the floor in front of their lockers and tugged on their yellow boots. Their boots matched. So did their yellow raincoats and yellow hats and yellow umbrellas.

"I wish it rained more often," said Peanut,

pulling her hat down over her ears. "I like wearing these matching outfits."

"Me, too," said Jilly. "I wish we had more outfits that matched." She struggled into her backpack. "Let's go."

Outside, the rain splattered them.

"I," said Peanut, splashing into a puddle, "love . . . splashing." She stamped into three more puddles.

Jilly closed her eyes and turned her face up to the rain. She hadn't even opened her umbrella. "I love the way rain feels on my face." She opened her eyes and looked up at the windows of the Learning Center. "Maybe if those men working on the roof hadn't started doing stuff last week, there wouldn't be water coming into the LC. Like Miss Kraft said."

"Maybe it would be worse," said Peanut, splashing into another puddle. "I heard Mr. Larson tell Miss Kraft that they wanted to fix the roof last fall, but it got cold too early."

They stopped at the corner, waiting for cars to pass.

Jilly fished coins out of her pocket and counted them. "I've got just enough to buy one of those red notebooks at the little store," she said. "Let's stop there."

The little store — that's what everyone called Grumbecks'. Mr. Grumbeck sold newspapers and magazines and school supplies and milk and apples and the small things people forgot to pick up at the big supermarkets.

"My mom made me throw away my gum last night when she saw me stick it under the rim of my dinner plate," said Peanut. "I could use some bubble gum."

They crossed the street and headed toward Grumbecks', walking slowly in the pattering rain.

"I loved the snow when it came last fall," said Jilly. "And now I like the rain. It means spring is practically here."

"It's been raining for three whole days," said Peanut. "I bet tulips and daffodils will start to come up."

They looked into the yards of the houses they passed. But there were no signs of green shoots reaching up out of the dark, rain-wet earth.

A bell above the door tinkled when they

went into Grumbecks'. Mr. Grumbeck was reading, his chair tipped back against the counter.

"Big fact," he said, looking up from his book, smoothing his bushy mustache with one finger. "It says here that birds have special languages. Think of that!"

"You mean," said Jilly, going to the notebook rack, talking over her shoulder, "like when a robin says *tweet-tweet* it means 'Hello, nice day,' but when she says *tooey-phweet* it means 'Look at this yummy worm'?"

"More than that." Mr. Grumbeck shook his head. "The *tweets* and *tooey-phweets* do mean special things. But what this fine book says is that robins and sparrows do not understand each other. Tsk." He shook his head again. "Just like people in different countries."

"Wow," said Jilly. "Wow!" Mr. Grumbeck was always finding wonderful things in the books he read. He called them big facts, and he had been telling them to her ever since she started to read. He seemed to have a big fact to tell her every time she came into the store. She tried to have big facts to trade back to him.

11

Peanut studied the boxes of bubble gum, listening. Mr. Grumbeck never offered big facts to her.

Jilly poked around in the back of her mind for a big fact. Then she thought of one she had read only yesterday. "Hippopotamuses," she said, "can open up their mouths almost four feet."

"Tsk!" said Mr. Grumbeck, his eyes wide. "Think of that!"

"Their mothers are always saying, 'Don't chew with your mouth open,'" said Peanut.

Mr. Grumbeck let out a low chuckle. It was the first time Peanut had ever heard him laugh — Mr. Grumbeck ought to laugh more often. "May I have one of those, please?" she asked, pointing.

Mr. Grumbeck, his book under his arm, got up and gave Peanut her bubble gum. She paid for it, and Jilly came with her notebook and gave Mr. Grumbeck the exact amount of change for it.

Mr. Grumbeck went back to his chair. He didn't even seem to hear the bell ring when Peanut and Jilly went outside.

"That's the first time I ever heard Mr. Grumbeck laugh," said Peanut. "I've been thinking he's kind of a grump — Mr. Grump-beck."

"He is not," Jilly protested. "You just haven't known him as long as I have. Start getting big facts for him, and he'll trade back. You'll see."

Peanut thought about that. It would be kind of fun to trade big facts with Mr. Grumbeck. Then she thought about him laughing. It would be even more fun to make him laugh.

CHAPTER 2

■▼■▼■▼■▼■▼■▼■▼■▼■▼■▼■▼■

The front stairway was roped off so that nobody could use the stairs. That was the first thing Peanut and Jilly saw when they got to school the next morning. What was going on?

Lots of the kids were crowded around the stairway, looking up, talking excitedly.

"Everybody has to use the back stairs."

"Mr. Larson said so."

"I heard the Learning Center's a big mess."

"Buckets of water got in there during the night."

"I heard the whole ceiling fell in."

"I heard Mrs. Harris got all wet."

14

"I heard that the ceiling fell down right on Mr. Granger's head."

"The penguin projects we made all got ruined with water."

"Water's heavy. They think the floor in the LC is going to cave in."

Jilly turned to Peanut. "Let's go look," she whispered.

Peanut checked out the big clock at the end of the hall. "We've got five minutes before the bell," she whispered back.

Quietly they moved away from the crowd and made their way to the north stairway. They didn't run, even though they were dying to.

The hallway was filled with kids pushing things into their lockers, calling to each other.

"I heard the fire department came during the night to pump out the water."

"I heard they're going to send us home. No school today."

"Oh, boy! Vacation!"

Doing a very good job of looking as though they weren't up to anything in particular, Peanut and Jilly reached the back stairway. Trying to look as though they belonged up on the second floor — which they did not — they climbed the stairs and headed down the hall toward the Learning Center. Kids had gathered there, too, standing as close to the entrance as they could get.

But there was nothing to see. Canvas covered the doorway. Sawhorses stood in front of the canvas to keep people out.

Cold air stirred the heavy cloth and touched Jilly's face. "Where is the air coming from?" she murmured.

"A big hole in the roof, maybe," said Peanut.

Thumping sounds came from behind the canvas. "What's going on in there?" Jilly asked.

Peanut moved close to Jilly so that their arms touched. They stared at the covered-up entrance, not talking. The rain had been so much fun yesterday, making puddles for splashing, tickling the earth to tease the daffodils into coming up. But today the rain was more like tears dropping out of the sky — sad. And scary, too, because it had come inside Alcott School where it did not belong and hurt the Learning Center. Could rain hurt people, too?

16

The bell rang, and Peanut and Jilly went down the back stairway, not talking, thinking their own thoughts. They hung their matching raincoats in their lockers and went into their room, closing the door behind them.

"Miss Kraft? Miss Kraft?" demanded Ollie. "Is it true school's shutting down, and we're all going to have to transfer to another school?"

"Good heavens!" said Miss Kraft. "How rumors fly! Believe me, you will not have to transfer to another school."

"Is Mr. Granger okay?" asked Erin. "I mean, did he have to go to the hospital when the ceiling fell on him?"

"Wherever in the world did you hear that?" said Miss Kraft. "No ceiling fell on Mr. Granger. I spoke with him a few minutes ago."

And then she went on to answer as many questions as she could. Yes, there were problems with the ceiling in the Learning Center. Yes, water had gotten in there — a lot of water. Nobody knew at this point how much damage there was. Mr. Granger and Mrs. Harris and the workers were looking things over right now.

"Let's get down to work," she said. She got all the groups started on their special projects while she worked with one of the reading groups in the corner under the windows.

It was not an easy morning. Peanut had trouble remembering the things she read about Benjamin Franklin — and she *liked* him. Jilly kept dropping her pencil and breaking the point and having to go to the pencil sharpener again and again.

Everybody looked up when the door opened and Mrs. Perrin came in. Mrs. Perrin was the school secretary. She always brought news of something different going on. Miss Kraft stood at the door talking with her, nodding. At last Miss Kraft closed the door and turned to the class.

"There will be an assembly in the gym," she said. "Put your things away and line up quietly. I said quietly," she called over the hubbub that followed.

They did their best to be quiet when they went to the gym.

Mr. Granger came in looking serious, not smiling. He didn't stop on his way up to the front to say funny things to people the way he usually did. All eyes were on him, and by the time he turned to face them, the gym was still. Then somebody sneezed.

"*Gesundheit,*" boomed Mr. Granger.

Everybody laughed.

"We have a problem," said Mr. Granger, looking around. "But not one we can't solve." He told them how the heavy rains of the past week had weakened the roof, how rain had collected in a gigantic puddle up there. "There came a moment," he said, "when our roof said, 'I'm tired, I'm feeling weak' — "

The little kids in the front rows giggled.

" — and just gave up. It sagged, and a hole opened up, and the puddle poured into the Learning Center. Unfortunately it occurred during the night, and the water had a lot of time to soak into things before Mrs. Harris arrived this morning and saw what had happened. But fortunately — and we must remember this — nobody got hurt."

So much for the rumors. Mr. Granger and Mrs. Harris were okay.

"Now," Mr. Granger continued, "there is

something you can do to help."

Everybody leaned forward.

"You can go back to your rooms and gather up your things — "

There was a stirring and rustling throughout the gym.

"Hold it," boomed Mr. Granger. "You are to clear your home situations with your teachers. Those of you who have an adult at home will be free to leave for the day. If your parents are at work, you are to remain here in one of the first-floor classrooms. Your teachers will fill you in on your activities for today."

"Can we help?" called one of the bigger boys at the back of the gym.

"Probably," said Mr. Granger. "But not today. School will re-open tomorrow morning, and I expect all of you to be here on time. Any more questions?"

"But what will we do later to help?" asked one of the bigger girls.

"I have an idea or two," said Mr. Granger. "I will fill you all in later. For today we simply have to assess the damage."

And so that was that. They filed out of the

gym and back to class. Miss Kraft gave out extra assignments in math and reading. And then, because Peanut's mother wasn't home, she gave Peanut permission to go to Jilly's house.

"The whole day!" said Peanut when they got outside. "Just to hang out. Neat!"

"After we finish the math and reading stuff," Jilly reminded her.

"That won't take long," Peanut said breezily. Her mind skipped to something else. "It's really nice to know your father is always at home when you're at school. It's kind of cozy." She was quiet for a moment, then added, "When we lived in Minneapolis, my mom was always home. Now that she's going to school, she's hardly ever there during the day."

"What's your mom going to be when she finishes school?" asked Jilly. It seemed strange, to think of a mother going to school to learn things, not to teach as Jilly's mother did.

"She's studying music," said Peanut.

"But she plays the piano better than anyone I ever heard," said Jilly. "Why does she have to study it some more?"

Peanut wasn't sure. "She studies other things, I guess. Anyway, she's going to have to go to school for a long time. Then, she says, maybe she will teach music."

They came to a puddle, but Peanut didn't stomp in it. "I liked things better in Minneapolis," she said softly.

"But we didn't know each other then," said Jilly.

Peanut brightened. "You're the second-best thing about living in Evanston," she said positively.

"Hey!" said Jilly. "You mean I'm not the very best? How do you like that!" she said to a tree, in passing. "I'm second best!"

"Nibbsie," said Peanut. Nibbsie was her dog. The thought of Nibbsie made her smile.

Jilly did sort of understand. After all, she had her cat, Bumpy.

"And after that," said Peanut, getting cheerier and cheerier, "I like having a room to myself, not having to share with Maggie. And those smile cookies from Maier's Bakery. And getting to go to the Field Museum. And maybe getting a brand-new bike when summer comes.

And being almost a year older. It gets me a year closer to twelve, and maybe then I can have my ears pierced."

She chattered all the way to Jilly's house, feeling better and better.

It was rather nice, being at the Matthewses' house during the day, with just the three cats to keep them company, and Mr. Matthews working in his art studio up on the top floor. They did their assignments and played rock music LOUD until Mr. Matthews came downstairs and said they had to turn it down because the plaster would soon be falling off the walls with all that noise.

He stayed downstairs for a while, and they ate lunch together. Jilly made peanut-butter-and-banana sandwiches, and Mr. Matthews said she was turning into a gourmet cook.

CHAPTER
3

The stairway was still roped off when Peanut and Jilly got to school the next morning. But there was something else to take their minds off the stairway and what might be going on upstairs. Carts stacked with books were strung out down the middle of the hall. A sign on one of the carts read ADOPT BOOKS. What did that mean?

"I'm adopted," said Courtney, joining Peanut and Jilly. "My mother said that she and my father chose me special and got to keep me forever."

"Are we going to get to choose these books

and keep them forever?" said Jilly in wonderment.

"I want *Charlotte's Web*," said Peanut. "I'd like to read that book every single week for the rest of my life."

Nate had been listening. "But if we all get to take the books, what will happen to the LC?" Nate worried a lot. "Does that mean we won't have a Learning Center anymore?"

Jilly's thoughts turned somersaults as she remembered all the things she had gone to the Learning Center to look up. How could you have a school without books and tapes and records and all the things that were part of a Learning Center?

"Aw, come on, Nate," said Peanut. "That won't happen!"

And yet, as one, they raced to their room, still wearing their raincoats. Miss Kraft would tell them what was happening.

They almost bumped into her, coming out the door. "Hold it, all of you," she said. "What are you doing coming in here in those wet clothes?"

The questions tumbled out.

"Why are all the books down here in the hall?"

"What does it mean, 'adopt books'?"

"What about the LC?"

"Won't there be one anymore?"

"We're going to find out about all that first thing this morning," Miss Kraft said calmly. "Now scoot and get out of those wet coats. You're dripping all over the floor. We'll go to the gym as soon as the bell rings."

They trailed off to their lockers. As they peeled off their wet things, Peanut looked around and saw that kids had started lining up outside other classrooms.

It seemed to take forever for everybody to get there. Best friends wanted to be with best friends, and some kids wanted to be first in line while others wanted to be last. But at last they marched to the gym.

Mr. Granger looked more cheerful than he had yesterday. Mrs. Harris was with him.

"We worked very late last night," he said, "and we decided on several things. Mrs. Harris will tell you the first part of our plan."

28

"You have seen the book carts in the hall," said Mrs. Harris.

A murmur ran through the gym.

"Each of you will be allowed to borrow as many books as you can carry and keep them until the Learning Center is back in operation."

Jilly's jumping-around thoughts settled down. There was still going to be a Learning Center.

"That means we have to bring them back," Courtney said softly. "That's not really adopting. What it is, is borrowing books for a long time."

"I'm going to adopt the whole encyclopedia," Nate said seriously. "Maybe I can bring my little brother's wagon to school to take the books home."

Mrs. Harris was still talking. ". . . today. We will begin with the youngest children and work our way up to the top classes. Your teachers will sign out the books you choose. Now remember, you will be responsible for them. Treat them well."

Mr. Granger spoke up. "Teachers, please allow your people to keep their adopted books in your classrooms until the rain clears up. I understand sunshine is predicted for tomorrow. Now" — he paused, looking around — "about damage from our deluge."

Everyone leaned forward.

"Unhappily," he went on, "some books are beyond repair. Too much water soaked into them, and they cannot be saved." He named a number of books. "Our shelf of encyclopedias was among them," he finished.

Nate's face fell.

Things sounded pretty bad.

"Why is Mr. Granger looking so cheerful?" whispered Peanut.

"He smiled when he started talking," Jilly whispered back.

"But all is not lost," Mr. Granger said. "Now for the second part of our plan.

"Workers are upstairs right now closing up the opening in the roof, making it watertight and strong. Once the roof is solid, the Learning Center will be replastered, repainted, and a new floor will be laid down. And then you will bring back your adopted books. That brings me to part three of our plan.

"Members of the parents' group were here last night, helping us. They have already started thinking about fund-raising activities to replace the damaged books. I heard talk about bake sales and car washes. There was even something about a jacks contest."

"Jacks!" exploded Ollie. "That's *little* kid stuff!"

Mr. Granger went right on talking. "Our Learning Center is going to be as good as new, and fairly soon, too. As a sign of my promise, I will let my beard grow until the day we move back in. You can all watch me shave it off."

Laughter filled the gym.

"All right!" The voice came from somewhere at the back, among the older kids.

"Way to go!" called Elvis.

"Where are you gonna shave it?" called Ollie.

"You decide," laughed Mr. Granger. "You tell me."

Suggestions came from all sides.

"Here in the gym?"

"In your office?"

31

"We can't all get in there to watch. Get real, Dumbo."

"Why not in the Learning Center?"

In a pause in the chatter, Peanut's voice carried clearly through the gym. "What about out on the front steps?"

"Yeah!" "Right!" "Great idea!" "Out on the steps."

CHAPTER
4

"Don't tell me what he decided," said Mr. Matthews. He was hunched over his drawing board inking a drawing of a horse leaping over a fence. Peanut and Jilly perched on tall stools beside him, watching. "Let me tell you," he said. "He decided that he'll stand on his head on the roof to shave off his beard."

"Oh, Daddy, you're being silly!" said Jilly. "If he was up on the roof, we couldn't see him, and if he stood on his head, he wouldn't have his hands free to shave. And besides, his beard would flop all over his face and into his eyes. And — "

"On the front steps," Peanut put in, laughing. "He said he'll shave off his beard out on the front steps."

"It was Peanut's idea, and everybody thought it was great," said Jilly, proud of Peanut for having such a super idea. "And we had another idea, too. We're going to earn money to buy books."

Mr. Matthews cleaned his pen on a tissue and leaned back in his chair. "How are you going to do that? Well . . . I suppose you can do odd jobs around here. Mom would like that."

Jilly wrinkled her nose. She hated odd jobs around the house. "Nope. Better than that. More fun. We're going to have a run-a-thon."

"A what-a-thon?" asked Mr. Matthews.

"You know," Peanut explained, "like where you get somebody to sponsor you and pay you to run lots of miles. And then we'll give the money to Mrs. Harris to buy books."

"Not a bad idea," said Mr. Matthews. "Who thought that up?"

Peanut and Jilly spoke together. "David." "Elvis."

"David thought about earning money first."

"But Elvis thought about the run-a-thon when he adopted that book about the Olympics."

"Yes, but David was the one who thought of getting people to give us money to do the running."

"Miss Kraft is going to talk to Mr. Granger about it and see if it's okay for us to do that."

"Daddy?" The voice came from downstairs. "I'm home. I'm coming up there."

"Right, sport," called Mr. Matthews. He got up and went to the top of the stairs to meet Jackie.

Peanut and Jilly stayed at the drawing board. "I'm going to ask my grandma and grandpa to sponsor me," said Peanut. "If Mr. Granger says the run-a-thon is okay. I'm going to ask Mrs. McCune, too." Peanut had baby-sat with the McCune twins.

"We're going to have to go around asking people," said Jilly. The very thought made her want to run and hide under her bed. She would do it, though. She would! "I'll ask Mr. and Mrs. Oliver, our neighbors," she said, thinking. But — who else could she ask?

Peanut guessed how Jilly was beginning to feel. "We can go around together," she said comfortingly. "You know — you come with me when I ask Mrs. McCune, and I'll go with you when you ask Mrs. Oliver."

Friends were wonderful — that's what Jilly thought. Friends stood up for each other when things were rough.

Mr. Matthews came back to the drawing board with Jackie riding piggyback. "We're low on milk," he said to Jilly. "I didn't get to the supermarket today. How about running to the little store and picking up some?"

He fished around in his pocket for money while Jackie squealed, still clutching him around his neck. He handed the money to Jilly.

Jackie slid to the floor. "Can I go? I want to go with Jilly."

Jilly loved her little brother dearly. But it wasn't always fun having him tagging along after her, having to look out for him.

Mr. Matthews took care of that problem. "But if you go with Jilly, sport, I'll be alone here. I don't think I want to be alone."

"Okay," Jackie agreed, proud to be needed. "I'll stay here with you, Daddy. What did you draw today?" he asked, climbing onto his father's chair to check out the drawing board. "I want to see what you drew."

"Better get moving while the moving's good," Mr. Matthews suggested in a low voice.

Jilly took his advice.

"I can't go with you," Peanut informed Jilly when they got outside. "I have to go home and let Nibbsie out."

They parted at the corner, and Jilly jogged the rest of the way to the little store. If she was going to be in a run-a-thon, she'd better start practicing. If, that is, Mr. Granger said they could in fact have the run-a-thon.

Mr. Grumbeck looked up from his book as soon as she came into the store. "Big fact," he said. "Earthquakes. One happened right here in the Midwest in eighteen eleven. One great, big, huge earthquake. I just read that."

"Wow!" said Jilly. She hadn't known there could be earthquakes any place but in California. Should she worry about it? Eighteen eleven was a long time ago. . . . She decided not to worry and went to the cooler, thinking about which of her big facts she could give Mr. Grumbeck in trade. Monkeys' tails? No. That was an especially good one, and she was saving it for a while. Dinosaurs, she decided.

She carried the milk to the counter. "The last dinosaurs died more than sixty million years ago. They all just died practically at once, and then there weren't any more. Nobody knows why."

"Tsk," said Mr. Grumbeck. "Think of that! Where did you learn that?"

"In a book in our Learning Center," said Jilly. Suddenly she remembered that the book about dinosaurs was one that had been ruined. She told Mr. Grumbeck about the flood.

"Tsk," Mr. Grumbeck said again. Mr. Grumbeck seemed to like that sound, *tsk*. He said it a lot. "Now that's a sad fact."

"So I guess I can't tell you any more about dinosaurs," said Jilly. "Not until the Learning Center gets all fixed and I can look things up." She had another thought. "I've got some big facts, but not a whole lot. Maybe I'll run out of big facts and won't be able to trade."

"You've got good credit here in this store," said Mr. Grumbeck. "I will put big facts you owe me on your bill. You can pay up when you get your Learning Center place fixed. Okay?"

"Okay," Jilly agreed.

Was there, she wondered as she jogged home with the milk, anybody else in the whole world who could charge big facts and pay up later? Well, she still had the one about the monkeys.

CHAPTER
5

■ ■ ■ ■ ■ ■ ■ ■ ■ ■
■ ■ ■ ■ ■ ■ ■ ■ ■

The next day everybody picked out armloads of books from the carts in the hall, and Peanut did get to adopt *Charlotte's Web*. And everybody chattered like mad about Mr. Granger's beard. What was he going to look like? They eyed him closely when he walked down the hall. He didn't have a beard yet, but he looked sort of scruffy. That's the word Courtney used — scruffy.

"How long does it take to grow a beard?" asked Erin. "Does it grow, like, a foot in a week? Is Mr. Granger going to look like Rip van Winkle pretty soon?"

"Dumbo!" said Ollie. "Your hair doesn't grow a foot a week, does it?"

Erin looked confused. "Are beards like head hair, then?"

"Don't you call Erin Dumbo, Ollie Burke," Emmy said hotly. "How can she know about beards? She lives with her mother, not her father."

"How do we know Mr. Granger is really going to have a beard?" wondered Jilly. "I mean, he has hardly any hair up on top of his head."

Peanut didn't think that mattered. "Men always have beards," she said positively.

But they set up a beard watch, just the same. Everybody was going to keep a close eye on Mr. Granger's chin to see if his beard really was growing.

In the days that followed, big trucks brought loads of building stuff into the schoolyard, and workers tramped around on the roof and upstairs in the Learning Center. The sounds of pounding and thumping and whirring tools came from the second floor as some parents — a whole lot of them — had their first bake sale. All of the grown-ups in and around school bought bread and cookies and cakes. The kids went around munching on brownies.

The grass turned green, which meant that spring had really come. And Mr. Granger's chin got fuzzier and fuzzier, which proved that his chin was not as bald as the top of his head.

The best thing that happened, though, was that Mr. Granger did give permission for the run-a-thon. He even said that he and Mrs. Harris had decided that the new books would have bookplates in them with the names of the people who sponsored runners in the run-a-thon.

The day was set — a Saturday. The PTA said they would monitor the course and set the rules and help out at the checkpoints. The kids all began jogging wherever they went — except in the halls — getting into shape. And they all started thinking about sponsors to back them.

"My Uncle Woody said he'll back me," said Elvis. "My Aunt Loretta said she'll think about it. I bet she will, too."

43

They were in line in the cafeteria, stacking their trays after lunch.

"I asked the guy who delivers laundry," said David, "but he said no because he doesn't get paid enough money to do that. So then I went to the laundry and asked the owner, and he said he'd back me. I'm gonna ask the owner of the gas station where my dad buys gas, too."

"My mom's going to sponsor me," said Erin. "She's going to get me a new sweatsuit. I want it to be pink."

"Aren't you going to get somebody plus your mother?" asked Courtney. She counted off backers on her fingers. "Both my grandpas, that's two. And my Uncle Jack, and my parents' bridge club, and my parents. That's a whole lot, and I might get more."

"Have you asked anyone yet?" Peanut whispered to Jilly.

"My dad," Jilly whispered back. "But I haven't asked anybody else." How was she going to work up the nerve to ask the Olivers? She kept putting it off.

"My mom said yes," said Peanut. "I'm going

to ask Mrs. McCune today after school. Come with me."

Jilly brightened. She would watch Peanut and see what she did. And then maybe she would go right home and march up the Olivers' steps and knock on the door and ask Mrs. Oliver.

They went straight to the McCunes' after school, without even stopping at the Buttermans' to let Nibbsie out for a run. Peanut rang the doorbell. The sound of shrieking came from inside, and the twins, Bridget and Deirdre, pressed their noses to the living room window, waving and laughing.

The door opened.

"Why, Polly," said Mrs. McCune. "And Jilly. How nice to see you. Come in."

The twins ran into the hall and flung themselves at Peanut, yelling "Up, up, up," wanting to be picked up.

Peanut couldn't pick up both of them at the same time. They were getting too big for that. And she knew better than to pick up one and not the other. She knelt and hugged them.

"Such big girls," she said. Hearing herself talking to toddlers that way, she thought, Why, I sound like a grown-up!

"Did you come to tell us a story?" demanded one of the twins.

"Come see my teddy bear. He's sick with the lumps," demanded the other.

Jilly hid a laugh behind her hand. Lumps! Bridget — or was it Deirdre — must mean mumps!

Mrs. McCune saved Peanut from storytelling. She put her hand to her ear. "I think I hear your bears calling you," she said. "I think maybe their lumps are hurting and they need you."

The twins looked alarmed and darted back to the living room to check on the health of their teddy bears.

"Milk?" offered Mrs. McCune. "A cookie?"

Peanut would have loved a cookie. McCune cookies were the best in the neighborhood. But Nibbsie was waiting at home. He was probably barking and jumping at the door, wanting to go out. She turned down the offer of a cookie, and this time she didn't know how grown-up she sounded. She explained why there wasn't time. "But I was wondering," she said, "would you be a sponsor for me in our book run-a-thon?"

She went on to tell what that was. "You'll get to have your name in a book."

"What a great idea," said Mrs. McCune. "Of course you can count on Malachy and me." Malachy was Mr. McCune. "Just let me know what we have to do and when."

She held the door for them, and they got outside without another onslaught by the twins.

"See?" said Peanut when the door closed behind them. "Nothing to it."

Was it going to be that easy? Maybe, thought Jilly, she could manage to talk the way Peanut did when she went to see Mrs. Oliver.

There was a thumping at the window. They turned and saw the twins holding up their teddy bears. The bears had Band-Aids on their noses.

Jilly giggled. "I didn't know Band-Aids cured the mumps." She blew a kiss at the twins and they waved their bears' arms at her.

"Okay," said Peanut. "Let's go get Nibbsie.

And then it's your turn. I'll go with you to the Olivers' house."

Peanut had been right. Nibbsie was waiting for them, barking. He scrambled past Peanut and out into the yard with hardly a yippy hello.

Peanut closed the door, tried it to be sure it was locked, and she and Jilly followed Nibbsie. They had to run to keep up with him. Jilly always thought it strange that a dog as small as Nibbsie could run so fast that people had to race to keep up with him. After all, people's legs were lots longer than Nibbsie's. . . .

They went to the park, where Nibbsie stopped to say hello to Mr. Fanning's Irish setter, and then they turned toward Jilly's house. The Olivers lived right next door.

Jilly took a deep breath and headed up the walk, with Peanut and Nibbsie trailing behind her. The Olivers had some very interesting bushes that Nibbsie stopped to explore as Jilly mounted the steps. She rang the bell and waited. Peanut came up the steps to stand beside her, holding Nibbsie who had settled down and was resting quietly in her arms.

Mrs. Oliver peeked out through the window beside the door and then opened it, wiping her hands on a towel. "Oh, Jilly," she said, "you're the answer to a prayer. I'm in the middle of making apple pies for my bridge club tonight, and I'm low on sugar. Would you run to the little store and get some for me?"

Well, of course Jilly would! She often ran errands for Mrs. Oliver.

But first there was something to be attended to. "Mrs. Oliver," she said, remembering Peanut talking to Mrs. McCune, "we're running a book-a-thon at — "

"A what?" asked Mr. Oliver.

"A book-a-thon — hey, that's neat," said Peanut.

Jilly felt her face get red. "It's a *run*-a-thon to buy *books*," she corrected herself. And now she was rattled. She forgot all about sounding like Peanut and went on, sounding just like herself. "We get backers to pay us for the miles we run, and then we give the money to the Learning Center to buy books because so many got ruined in the flood," she finished in a rush.

"Why, of course I'll sponsor you, dear," said

50

Mrs. Oliver, "and you can tell me all about it after you come back with the sugar. I'll get my purse." She disappeared into the hall, came back, and tucked money into Jilly's pocket. "A pound should do," she said. "And you may keep the change to buy an ice-cream cone.

"Hurry back," she called as Jilly and Peanut started down the steps. "I really must get my pies into the oven."

"See?" said Peanut as they headed toward the little store. "That wasn't so hard."

Jilly felt good. The asking part was over. Now it would be easy to tell Mrs. Oliver about all the rest. And she knew what she was going to do with the "change" to buy an ice-cream cone. She was going to give it to the run-a-thon. Maybe she could do other errands for Mrs. Oliver and earn more "change." Maybe she could earn enough to buy a whole book!

Peanut couldn't go into the little store because Nibbsie was with them. She waited outside, tossing a stick for Nibbsie to retrieve while Jilly went inside for the sugar.

The bell above the door announced her arrival.

"Good," said Mr. Grumbeck. "I've been waiting for you to come in. Big fact. A volcano in the Pacific Ocean once blew up with such a bang it sent a tidal wave halfway around the world to Africa. The volcano was on an island called Krakatoa. Think of that!"

"Tsk!" said Jilly. She was beginning to sound like Mr. Grumbeck! "Think of that!" She got the sugar and took a quick peek into her big facts notebook. Two big facts. She would keep the monkey one for last. "Did you know," she asked, "that the earth gets heavier every year? A hundred thousand pounds heavier. It's from meteor dust coming from outer space."

"Now that," said Mr. Grumbeck, "is one huge fact. How do they know that? Is there some big scale where they weigh the earth every year?"

"I read about it in a book at school," said Jilly. "But I can't remember how they know." Why hadn't she thought to wonder about that? "I guess I'll have to charge it until we get all our books back in the Learning Center."

"I won't let you forget," said Mr. Grumbeck. "See? I'm writing it down here." And he did, looking businesslike and serious.

Jilly gathered up the sugar and her change and went back outside, fingering the coins, wondering how much it would take to pay for a book for the library.

Nibbsie fooled Peanut. Instead of taking the stick to her to throw, he brought it to Jilly.

"Hey!" yelled Peanut. "Whose puppy are you, anyway? Watch it, or I'll forget to feed you tonight."

Nibbsie paid no attention. He ran for the stick that Jilly tossed.

CHAPTER
6

■▄■▄■▄■▄■▄■▄■▄■▄■▄■

Peanut and Jilly could scarcely believe all the things that happened in the weeks following the flood. Word about the run-a-thon got around school because everyone in Miss Kraft's class talked so much about it. The little kids said they didn't see why they couldn't be part of it. Then the big kids wanted in, too. Soon everybody jogged to and from school. They jogged around the schoolyard while they waited for the doors to open. There were joggers all over the place. The boys were very serious about it. They puffed out their cheeks every time they breathed out because somebody said that's what marathon runners did.

Mr. Granger's beard got longer and bushier until it covered his chin and the sides of his face. And it was red! Everybody stopped to talk with him when he was in the halls. He didn't mind when they asked him questions about his beard. He told them he had not known it would be red because he had never grown a beard before.

One of the little kids learning how to use a ruler wanted to measure Mr. Granger's beard. Mr. Granger said that rulers were good for drawing lines, but he himself drew the line at letting anyone measure his beard.

The little kid didn't get the joke about drawing lines. But Peanut and Jilly, who were standing nearby, did, and they laughed along with Mr. Granger.

Pounding and thumping and rolling noises still came from the second floor. Mrs. Harris caught Ollie and Elvis behind the canvas "wall" at the entrance to the Learning Center, right inside the room. She sent them to the office to see Mr. Granger. He gave them a good talking to about staying out of dangerous places.

At lunch that day everybody crowded around Ollie and Elvis, asking questions. Ollie said that it looked as though the ceiling was back in one piece. Elvis said that half the new floor was finished. But they both agreed that the Learning Center was still sort of a mess.

One of the big things that happened in those weeks was the day the mothers came to school and had a jacks contest. They met in the gym at the end of the school day, and they sat on the floor like little kids and played jacks. People who wanted to watch had to stay behind a line of chairs near the door.

"Sometimes parents do the most embarrassing things," Peanut murmured to Jilly. "I mean, acting like little kids!"

"Don't tell anyone that this was all my mom's idea," Jilly whispered back. "I'll totally die if everyone finds out!"

"My mom said she thinks it's too bad I don't play jacks," said Peanut. "I told her I outgrew that game a million years ago."

"Look," said Jilly. "Your mom's doing Around the Moon."

Peanut watched for a moment and groaned. "She dropped one, and she was only on foursies. She should have practiced. I hate to say this, but she's not a very good jacks player."

"But she's laughing," said Jilly. "Do you suppose you forget how to play jacks when you get old?"

Emmy and Erin came to stand beside them.

"How is playing jacks going to make money to buy books?" asked Erin.

Neither Peanut nor Jilly quite understood that.

"I think," said Emmy "everybody pays to get into the contest. I heard my mom talking to Mrs. Genaro on the phone."

The contest went on and on, with first one mother dropping out, and then another. Mrs. Butterman did not make it to the final rounds. At last just three mothers remained — Mrs. Matthews was one of them. Mrs. Cramer, Courtney's mother, was the second, and the third was Mrs. Genaro, the mother of one of the boys in another class.

Mrs. Genaro lost on Eggs in the Basket sixes. Then it was a game between Mrs. Cramer and Mrs. Matthews. Mrs. Matthews didn't manage to scoop up all the jacks on her turn, but Mrs. Cramer did. She was the winner.

Courtney went to stand beside her mother and got to hold the winner's certificate. She looked hugely proud.

"Mom," moaned Jilly, "how could you lose! It's such a baby game!"

"Oh, honey," laughed Mrs. Matthews, "it's only a game. And it was fun while it lasted. And listen — I think we took in enough money to buy at least ten new books. Think of that!"

Jilly had to admit that the jacks contest hadn't been such a bad idea after all. Even though her mother had lost.

"I'd forgotten how much fun childhood games can be," said Mrs. Butterman as they walked home. "Maybe we can think of another one. Remember Double Dutch? How about a rope-skipping contest?"

"I can't stand it!" Peanut whispered to Jilly, and they ran on ahead so they wouldn't be embarrassed by listening.

The car washes put on by the PTA were not, at least, embarrassing. Peanut and Jilly went through the line twice, once with Jilly's mother in the Matthewses' car, and once with Peanut's mother in the Buttermans' car.

Lots of the kids were helping the parents. Peanut put her face right up to the car window and made a face at Ollie. Ollie turned the hose on the window. It made a loud smacking sound that Peanut was not expecting, and she jumped back, giggling. Ollie stood outside laughing at her.

Everybody in class had picked up more backers for the run-a-thon.

"Remember Mr. Fanning who owns the Irish setter?" Peanut asked Jilly. "He's always running Macushla when I take Nibbsie to the park. Well, I saw him at the park the other morning, and he said he would back me. And then I thought of somebody else. Remember how David got all those people where his parents shop? Well, I asked the manager at the supermarket, and he said he would."

Jilly had her father, of course, and Mrs. Oliver. And Mrs. Potter.

Jackie was all excited about the run-a-thon because he said he wanted there to be lots of books when he started going to Louisa May Alcott. Without even asking Jilly, he had asked Mrs. Potter to back her, and he brought word home that Jilly was supposed to go talk to her. Jilly had. And that's how she got her third backer.

She had done more errands for Mrs. Oliver, and she had saved almost a dollar and a half. Maybe she could back herself. Could a runner do that?

She was thinking about it the afternoon she went on still another errand to the little store. Mrs. Oliver had a perfectly terrible memory. She was always forgetting things. Today Jilly had to buy the vanilla Mrs. Oliver needed for her cake.

As usual, Mr. Grumbeck was reading.

Jilly was ready for him. "I've got a really big fact," she said as she came in the door. It was her last big fact.

"You don't say," said Mr. Grumbeck. "You tell me that big fact, and then I'll be as smart as you are."

"You know how monkeys hang by their tails?" she asked. "Well, only monkeys that live in South America can do that. Monkeys that live in Africa can't."

"Tsk," said Mr. Grumbeck. "Think of that."

Jilly set the bottle of vanilla on the counter and dug the money for it out of her jeans. "Now that's the last big fact I've got," she said. "I can't tell you any more. Not until the Learning Center opens up again."

"Tsk," said Mr. Grumbeck. "Terrible. When is that going to happen? When are you kids going to have your running contest?"

"Saturday," said Jilly. "Next Saturday."

"Tsk," said Mr. Grumbeck. "My feelings are hurt, you know. You didn't ask your old friend Grumbeck to back you. Everybody is backing a kid. But me? Nobody asked me. Tsk."

Jilly looked at him, surprised. Why hadn't she thought of asking Mr. Grumbeck? He read more books than anybody she knew.

"But," she said, dismayed, "but — I never thought about asking you. I mean, would you? I mean, would you back me? You'll get your name in a book in the Learning Center."

Mr. Grumbeck bowed slightly in a gracious way. He smoothed his mustache with a finger. "I would be pleased to back you," he said. "I will be your sponsor."

A nice, friendly, warm sort of feeling washed over Jilly. "Wow, Mr. Grumbeck," she said, "that's the nicest thing anybody has said to me all day."

She was outside on the street before she realized something. Mr. Grumbeck hadn't given her a big fact.

She ran back up the steps and opened the door a crack. Mr. Grumbeck was already deeply buried in his book. "You owe me a big fact, Mr. Grumbeck," she called.

"Put it on my bill," said Mr. Grumbeck. "Next time, I will pay you with an extra big fact."

CHAPTER
7

■■■■■■■■■■■■■■■■■■■■■■■■

Mr. Matthews and Jilly's brother Jerry weren't in the kitchen when Jilly ran downstairs on the morning of the big run-a-thon. They had gone to the park early to help get things ready.

Jilly looked at the orange juice and scrambled eggs and toast waiting at her place at the table. Ugh! She was too excited to eat! Then she thought about the morning ahead. A person needed lots of energy for a run-a-thon. I will, she told herself sternly, eat every single bite. She sipped her juice. It was cold and sweet and good. Then she tackled the eggs.

Her mother came to the table to keep her

64

company. She poured tea for herself. "Jackie wanted to watch the run-a-thon with Mrs. Potter. She's already been here to pick him up. He is so proud of you. Be sure to wave when you pass him."

"I wonder if Mr. Grumbeck will be there," said Jilly. The toast and eggs did taste rather good. "I mean, if he comes to the run-a-thon, who will sell things at the little store?"

Mrs. Matthews shook her head. She didn't know, either. "I have enormous admiration for Mr. Grumbeck," she said. "When he found out I'm a teacher, he told me that he had to leave school in the sixth grade to help support his family when his father died. That was in Europe. But he reads so much that he could put some college graduates to shame. He is truly an educated man — a self-educated man."

"We trade big facts," said Jilly.

"Big facts?" asked her mother.

"Tell you later," said Jilly. She gulped the last of her milk. "Got to go."

"Mrs. Oliver and I will be at one of the crossings," said Mrs. Matthews. "We'll be watching for you."

Peanut was outside her house, waiting for Jilly. "Hurry up, slowpoke," she called. As Jilly drew near, she added. "I'm so excited I could fly instead of running."

They headed for the park, not flying, but at a down-to-earth trot.

The park was already teeming with excited, chattering, laughing kids. Many of them had numbers pinned on their backs.

"Look. There's Elena," said Jilly, pointing. "I guess her ankle is okay." Elena had sprained her ankle playing tetherball on Wednesday. "She was scared she wouldn't be able to come today."

Emmy and Erin came running.

"Quick," Emmy gasped. "Get in line for your number. We've got ours already. Over here, over here." She herded them toward a line in front of several tables.

"I'm so glad it's not raining," burbled Erin. "I'd hate to get my new outfit sopping wet." She twirled to show them her new pink warm-up outfit. Erin got more and prettier new clothes than any girl in class.

Ollie strutted past them. He already had his

number. "Us guys," he said, "are gonna get back here to the starting place while you girls are still running the first block out."

"Aw, come on, Oll," said Peanut. "We're not racing for time. The point is staying in for the whole thing. That's what the backers are paying us for."

"Guys," Ollie insisted in the most infuriating Ollie way, "are better runners than girls."

"Know something?" Jilly said quietly. "You may run fast. But the big kids in the upper grades will run even faster. Even the girls," she added.

Ollie had no answer for that. Big kids . . . faster runners . . . what Jilly said might be true.

The line had been moving forward as they talked, and Jilly suddenly found herself facing her father and Jerry. They were pinning cards with numbers on them onto the backs of the runners. One of the mothers was writing names and numbers on a big sheet of paper. She listed backers' names under the runners' names.

"Do the Matthews family proud, scout," said

Mr. Matthews. "I'll be rooting for you. Number thirty-six," he called to the woman at the table. "Jillian Matthews."

"How're you doin', Goober?" asked Jerry, fastening Peanut's number to the back of her sweatshirt. "Number thirty-seven," he called. "Goober — "

"You stop that, Jerry Matthews," said Peanut. She hated being called Goober. "My name is *Polly* Butterman."

"Number thirty-seven, Polly Butterman," called Jerry. "Think your sister Maggie will be around here today?"

Jerry and Maggie sort of liked each other. Should Peanut tell him? After him calling her Goober? She had a sudden idea. "Tell you what, Jerry Matthews. You stop calling me Goober, and I'll tell you."

Jerry laughed. "You got it, Polly."

"Peanut," Peanut corrected him. "I think Maggie and my mom are going to watch us at Burnham Place."

"Way to go!" said Jerry. "See you around." He went to the next person in line.

Peanut and Jilly inspected each other's numbers and then jogged in place. They felt grown-up and important. Parents were standing around among the kids, but it was special to be one of the runners.

Miss Kraft came through the crowd, dressed for running. One by one her class gathered around her.

"Now remember," she said. "We are to stay on the sidewalks. And there will be an adult at every crossing. We will stay together as a class."

Ollie grumbled under his breath about beating the girls.

"Miss Kraft?" called Carrie. She pointed at some first-graders. "Those little kids can't run the whole way!"

"Of course not," said Miss Kraft. "But they are part of our school, too. They will run a short course right here in the park."

"Ahem!" Mr. Granger's voice sounded above all the laughter and talk. He was speaking into a bullhorn. His red beard stood out all around his face. "Ahem! Students of Louisa May Alcott School, today is Run-a-thon Day!"

"Yaaaay!" Cheers drowned him out.

"Quiet," boomed Mr. Granger.

"Shhh." "Quiet." "Shhh." Hushing noises sifted through the crowd.

"We will begin with the oldest group. They will have a three-minute lead on the class that follows them. There will be three-minute intervals between classes. Remember, now — you must stay together, each class together."

"Rats!" groaned Ollie.

"Oliver?" called Miss Kraft. "You are to follow the rules."

Mr. Granger was still talking. "Your teacher or another adult will be in charge of your class. They are your coaches. Their word is law."

"I'm glad Miss Kraft is running with us," Peanut whispered to Jilly.

"She'll be lots more fun than some stranger," Jilly agreed.

Mr. Granger was finishing his speech. ". . . back here in the park. Ready?" He raised his hand. The park became so silent that the twittering of a bird sounded loud. Then he blew a whistle, dropped his hand, and the first group moved on out. A cheer followed them.

CHAPTER
8

■▼■▼■▼■▼■▼■▼■▼■▼■▼■

One by one, at the sound of Mr. Granger's whistle, the classes trotted out of the park. Peanut thought their turn would never come. Everybody jiggled around, bouncing in place. But at last their class reached the head of the line.

Mr. Granger's whistle sounded, and they began, at last, to move. They headed north along Sheridan Road. The boys, with Ollie and Elvis leading, sprinted ahead of the class to set the pace and show the girls what great runners they were.

"Slow down, boys," called Miss Kraft. "We need an easy gait if we are going to stay the whole course."

"Rats!" someone — who? — called. But the boys did slow down to match Miss Kraft's pace.

Friends ran with friends. Emmy and Erin

were in front of Peanut and Jilly. Courtney and Elena were behind them.

Jilly turned and ran backward. "Is your ankle going to be okay, Elena? It isn't hurting, is it?"

Elena lifted her hand in an A-OK sign. "I'm fine," she said. "I'm glad my mother let me come. I was so scared she would say I couldn't. For three days I've been telling her my ankle is fine. I'd have died if I couldn't do this."

Cars on Sheridan Road slowed as people looked out at the crowd of runners, wondering what was going on. Clusters of people who did know waited along the way to see them pass.

A shrill yell met them at Kedzie Street. "Jilly! Jilly! Look at me, Jilly. I'm here."

Jackie was on the sidewalk ahead, jumping up and down, waving a flag. Jackie loved flags and waved them whenever he had the chance. Mrs. Potter stood behind him, smiling.

Jilly clasped her hands above her head. "Yeahhh, Jack-O," she called as they passed and was rewarded with one of Jackie's winning smiles. "Thanks again for backing me, Mrs. Potter," she called.

73

Peanut's mother and Maggie and Jerry were waiting at Burnham Place. "Way to go, Peanut!" "Right on!" called Maggie and Jerry.

Without breaking her stride, Peanut bowed dramatically.

Mrs. Butterman looked proud.

Miss Kraft moved from the front of the line to the back, encouraging them. "You're great kids. Did I ever tell you you're the best class I've ever taught?"

Now that was funny! Somebody had found out, and now everyone knew, that this was Miss Kraft's first year of teaching.

Parents stood at every street crossing, holding back the cars until each class group passed. And parents were at the checkpoints, stamping the runners' cards. The first stamp was a tree, the second a bear. There were going to be six stamps in all.

One group of parents had set up a lemonade stand. It was at the halfway mark. Miss Kraft said everybody had to stop for a minute or two for a drink, even though Ollie groaned a lot about it.

"This is so good," sighed Peanut, holding

out her paper cup for a refill. "Wouldn't it be terrible to die of thirst in the Sahara Desert?" The idea had just occurred to her. "I hope I never do that."

"If you were a camel, you wouldn't die of thirst," said Jilly. "Camels can go for days without drinking water." There! She had just suddenly remembered that big fact. She was going to have to tell Mr. Grumbeck — after she checked to find out exactly how many days, because he was sure to ask.

She held out her card for stamp number 3 — a butterfly — as Miss Kraft called, "Ready? Set. Let's go."

They moved on, dropping their cups into a wastebasket one of the parents held out.

They hadn't gone far — they were heading back to the park now — when a soft "ouch" sounded behind them.

Jilly swung around. "Elena? You didn't turn your ankle again, did you?"

Elena shook her head. But Jilly wasn't sure she could believe her.

"Should we get Miss Kraft?" asked Peanut. Elena was limping slightly.

"No," she wailed. "Don't tell. She'll make me drop out. Don't tell."

Word passed quietly along the line. Elena hurt her ankle again . . . hurt her ankle . . . hurt her ankle. Don't tell Miss Kraft . . . Miss Kraft . . . Miss Kraft.

Suddenly Peanut and Jilly found Ollie and Elvis running beside them.

"What's up?" muttered Elvis.

"Need some strong guys back here?" asked Ollie.

Peanut explained. "She's afraid Miss Kraft will make her drop out, and she doesn't want to."

"Leave it to us guys," said Ollie.

Before Courtney quite knew what was happening, she found herself elbowed aside and Ollie and Elvis trotting on either side of Elena. They each had a hand under her elbows.

"This will help," said Elvis.

"Take off some of the weight," said Ollie.

It did make a difference. Elena began to smile.

"Is something going on back there?" called Miss Kraft, looking over her shoulder. Elena flashed a radiant smile. "We're trying some-

thing different," she called. Which didn't quite answer Miss Kraft's question.

Miss Kraft looked at her sharply. Then, seeming to think that everything was fine, she jogged on ahead.

Suddenly lots of the kids began running in threes. Courtney fell back and joined Carrie and Beth. David appeared out of nowhere and joined Peanut and Jilly. And that's how they finished the run-a-thon. Every time Miss Kraft looked in their direction, Elena put on a big smile, and everybody around her laughed and joked.

"Know something?" asked Peanut as they jogged the long last block to the park. "I didn't think this was going to be such a big deal. I've walked this far lots of times. But right now I'd give anything to fall down on the grass and not move for a month."

Suddenly Jilly thought of breakfast — so long ago. "I," she said, "would give anything for something to eat right this very minute."

Peanut looked as though she had been struck by lightning. "No!" She slapped her forehead with her hand. "I can't believe it. This is the first time I have ever, ever heard you say that. Sometimes you make me feel terrible because you're never hungry, and I could always eat a horse."

"We made it!" Elena chortled from behind them. "We're here!"

One of the mothers stood at the entrance to the park, stamping their cards — a frog this time — as they passed her.

Jilly turned, looking from Ollie to Elvis. They had wanted to lead the class into the park. Instead, here they were not leading at all, and not seeming to mind, still helping Elena. "Know what I think?" she said. "Of the whole school, we've got the best kids in our class."

Miss Kraft heard her and smiled. "Well, didn't I tell you that?"

"Ollie's heart is bigger than his mouth," said Peanut. "And his mouth is awful big."

They went on into the park and flopped onto the grass under a tree. Lying flat on her back, Jilly looked up at the new leaves overhead. "I love the color of those leaves." Then she frowned. "Were they that color last year? I think they were darker green then."

Peanut wasn't sure. "Maybe they are lighter when they first come out."

"I'll have to watch," murmured Jilly. "I don't remember from last spring."

Mothers came around with paper cups and jugs of lemonade. Peanut and Jilly rested contentedly, sipping, watching as the rest of the classes came jogging into view.

"Ahem!" Mr. Granger's voice brought silence to the park. "Ahem! Welcome home, everybody."

A cheer went up.

"The rest of this beautiful Saturday belongs to you to do as you like," he said. "But first, a few announcements of interest to you. Ahem. The first class that went out today was the first class back here."

Everybody laughed. What had they expected?

"And the last class out was the last class back," someone called.

"Seriously," Mr. Granger went on. "Mr. Klemper's class had the most sponsors. Congratulations, Mr. Klemper's class."

"Awwww," moaned Courtney as everybody clapped because lots of sponsors meant lots of books for the Learning Center. "And I even had six sponsors. Awwwww."

"There is one other outstanding class among us," boomed Mr. Granger. "Only one class was entirely here, no absentees, no dropouts along the way. That is Miss Kraft's fine class. Let's give them a hand."

Everyone cheered. From their places stretched out on the grass, Miss Kraft's class lifted their arms and waved wearily.

"I will see you on Monday morning," boomed Mr. Granger. "The Learning Center will be back in business that day. That is the day you will return the books you adopted. All of them. Nobody is going to forget. Right?"

"Right . . . right . . . right," came the echoes from around the park.

"Mr. Granger?" somebody called. "Are you going to cut off your beard on Monday?"

Mr. Granger stroked his red beard. "You would have me shave off this innocent, beautiful beard that never harmed anyone?"

"Yes!" came the roar.

"Wait and see," said Mr. Granger. "Wait and see."

Even though the run-a-thon was over, Peanut and Jilly couldn't go straight home to lunch. They had to stop at the little store. Mr. Grumbeck hadn't been at the park. Jilly wanted to show him her card, to prove that she had run the whole way.

People were buying things when they went into the store. They had to wait while a boy bought bread, and a woman bought coffee. But at last the bell dinged, and the door closed behind them.

Mr. Grumbeck settled himself in his chair and tipped it back against the counter. "You find what you want and then bring it here," he said, looking longingly at his book as though he wanted to be reading, not talking to people.

"We didn't come to buy anything," said Jilly. "We just came to see you."

"You don't say," said Mr. Grumbeck. He looked pleased.

"Do say," said Jilly. "The run-a-thon is over.

We just finished. We ran the whole way, and our class was best, and the Learning Center is going to open on Monday, and there will be heaps of new books."

"You don't say," Mr. Grumbeck said again. "You did all that running around this morning, you must be hungry. Have an apple." He nodded toward a box in the window. "Over there."

Peanut and Jilly helped themselves. The apples were red and shiny and smelled wonderful.

"Big fact," said Mr. Grumbeck as they came back to him. "A run-a-thon is like a marathon. Okay? The first one of those was in Greece. It happened in 490 B.C."

"I've got a big fact for you," said Jilly. "Camels can go for days and days without drinking water."

"They drink a couple of gallons of water all at once," said Mr. Grumbeck. "Camels I know about."

Jilly sighed. She couldn't win them all. She couldn't always expect to top Mr. Grumbeck in the big facts game.

CHAPTER
9

■▼■▼■▼■▼■▼■▼■▼■▼■▼■

"I earned nearly seven dollars," Jilly told Peanut as they walked to school on Monday morning, their adopted books in their backpacks. "I've saved it all, and I'm going to give it to Mrs. Harris for a book."

"I didn't know you were doing that — earning money for a book," said Peanut. "How come you didn't tell me?"

"I didn't know how much I could really earn," said Jilly. And she added truthfully, "Or how much I could save."

"Nearly seven dollars," said Peanut, shifting her backpack, which was really heavy. "That sure is a lot. Listen — I thought I'd get to read *Charlotte's Web* every week while I had it. But I only read it three times. I hate to give it back."

Jilly decided then and there what she would give Peanut for her birthday. She tucked away the idea in the back of her mind. She pulled her backpack higher up onto her shoulders. "I wonder if this is how a camel feels," she wondered.

"If you feel like a camel," said Peanut, "spit on that crack in the sidewalk." She pointed. "I dare you. Camels spit with deadly accuracy. The guide at the zoo said so."

Jilly halted. She eyed the crack, screwed up her lips, and spit. She missed by a mile. "Big fact," she said. "People do not spit with deadly accuracy."

Courtney and Emmy and Erin came running to meet them, their own backpacks bouncing.

"I saw you!" said Courtney. "You spit!" She wrinkled her nose. "Double yuck. It's not polite to spit."

"I won't do it again," promised Jilly. "I was just acting like a camel."

Courtney sent her a long, funny look. "Sometimes I don't understand you at all, Jilly Matthews. I am not even going to ask why you were acting like a camel."

"Do you think Mr. Granger is really going to do it?" Erin asked breathlessly. "Shave off his beard?"

"He promised," Emmy said seriously. "He said he would when the Learning Center is done. He can't go back on a promise."

"The kids sure are bringing back the adopted books," said Peanut, looking around. People were coming from all directions, loaded down with books.

"I just hope he doesn't make us wait until the end of the day," sighed Erin. "I don't think I could stand it."

Jilly stood on her toes. Why were so many of the kids crowded around the steps? She peered past all the moving bodies and caught a glimpse of a table in front of the big doors. There were things on the table. Sunlight glinted off a mirror. She giggled. "He *is* going to do it. I think everything he needs to shave is on that table."

They plunged into the crowd, trying to get closer. No luck. They hopped up and down for a better view of the steps. It was still too hard to see past all the bobbing people standing there.

"We've got to get closer," said Peanut. "Come on." She wormed her way among the kids, moving toward the side of the crowd. Once there, she headed closer to the front rows near the steps.

"Here," she said. "This is better. Can you see?"

Jilly only had to look past two or three heads. She pointed at the table. "What's that mug for?"

"I bet Mr. Granger is going to drink his coffee while he shaves," said Erin.

At that moment, Mr. Granger stepped through the double doors. He was carrying a bowl and a Thermos jug, which he set on the table. Then he looked around. "Good morning, one and all," he boomed out.

"Good morning, Mr. Granger," called the crowd.

"I promised," Mr. Granger said, rubbing his

hands together, looking pleased, "that when the Learning Center was finished, I would shave off my beard. Your part of the bargain was to bring back your adopted books. Do you have them? Let's see a show of hands."

Hands went up from everybody in the crowd.

"Good," said Mr. Granger. "Raise your hands, those of you who have not brought your adopted books to school this morning."

Not a hand went up.

"Well, then," boomed Mr. Granger, "I guess I must be as good as my word."

He tucked a yellow towel around his neck, picked up the mug, and held it up. "Shaving mug," he said. "With soap in it."

"I guess he's not going to drink coffee," murmured Erin.

Mr. Granger held up a brush. "Shaving brush," he said. He held up the Thermos. "Warm water." He poured some into the mug and stirred around in it with the brush. He held up the brush, dripping with soapsuds. "Lather," he said. "Bubbles."

He sat down in the chair and rubbed the

lather from the shaving brush on his cheek. Then he seemed to remember something. "Ooops!" he said and wiped it off. "I seem to have forgotten something."

A groan lifted out of the crowd.

"I had a visitor this morning. We have been given a very special donation for our Learning Center. Mr. Grumbeck of Grumbecks' store came to see me. He said he wanted several books of what he called 'big facts' to be included in our Learning Center. He said one of you would tell me all about big facts — "

Tsk! Imagine! Think of that!

"Jilly!" gasped Peanut. "Mr. Grumbeck meant you. You've got to tell Mr. Granger about big facts books."

"Didn't I tell you Mr. Grumbeck is really nice?" said Jilly. "And he's smart, too. He's nearly as smart as my father."

"I am sure," Mr. Granger went on, "that we can find a number of big facts books that will satisfy Mr. Grumbeck." He picked up his mug and smeared more of the lather on his cheek. Then, again he wiped it away.

"Such a nice beard," he said mournfully. "A truly beautiful beard. Surely you don't want me to shave it off!"

"Yes, we do!" everybody roared. "Yes . . . we . . . do!"

Mr. Granger gave a long, sad sigh. "Goodbye, beard," he said, patting his chin. "You have to go because I am a man of my word."

He slathered soapy bubbles onto half of his face as the crowd standing before the steps watched intently.

People walking past the schoolyard stopped and stared.

Mr. Granger scraped the beard off half of his face. He began to look like the Mr. Granger they had always known.

"Shall I shave the rest?" he asked, pointing to the other side of his face. "Or shall I *save* it?"

"Shave it!" came the shout. "Shave it. You promised."

"So I did," said Mr. Granger. "Not half a promise. A whole promise." With that he lathered the rest of his face and scraped it off. At last he wiped off his face and stood up. "Okay?" he asked. "Am I a man of my word?"

A cheer rose from the crowd. The people on the sidewalk clapped.

Mr. Granger piled the shaving things onto the table and set it off to one side. "Come in, one and all," he said, opening the doors. "I hope you will enjoy our new Learning Center."

Peanut and Jilly were among the first through the doors.

"I can hardly wait to see the LC," said Peanut. "Do you suppose the new books will be there?"

"Some of them, maybe," said Jilly. "Maybe not all of them. But I bet they'll come pretty soon. And they will have our names in them because we ran in the big run-a-thon."

"We can go to the LC and visit our books," said Peanut.

"We'll grow up and go to upper school," said Jilly. "But our books will stay here, with our names in them."

"Kids will look at the books and wonder who Polly Butterman and Jillian Matthews are."

"We can come back to visit our books every year."

"Even when we get to high school. And college."

"I'm going to art school, not college."

"But we can still be friends and come back to visit our books together."

"That's a fact. A big fact!"